LEXINGTON PUBLIC LIBRARY

W9-CMA-938

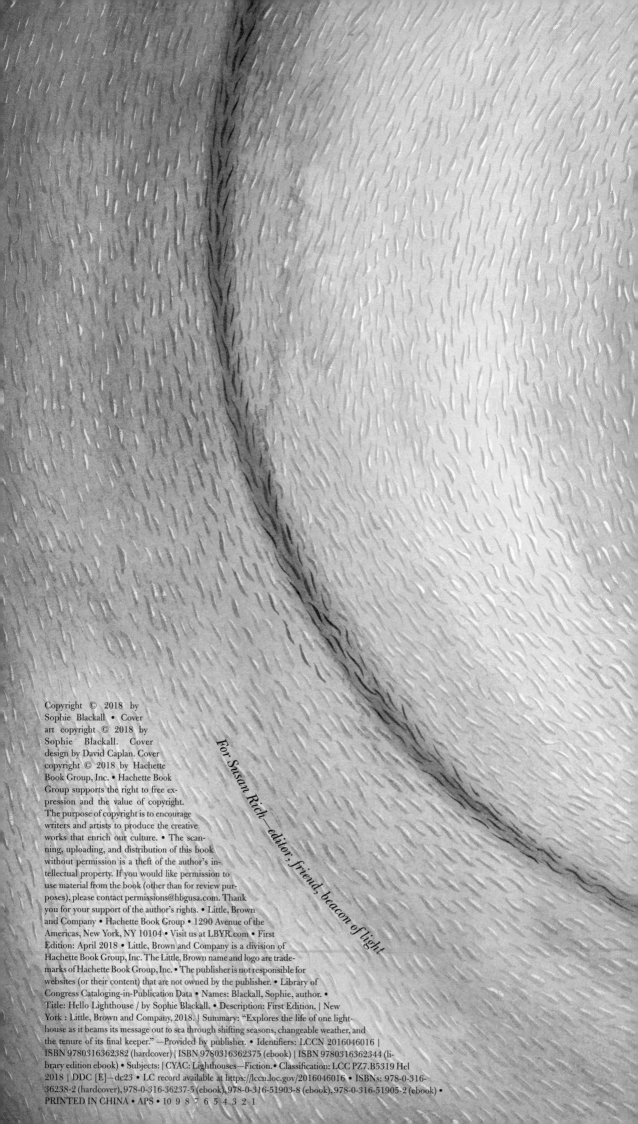

Copyright © 2018 by
Sophie Blackall • Cover
art copyright © 2018 by
Sophie Blackall. Cover
design by David Caplan. Cover
copyright © 2018 by Hachette
Book Group, Inc. • Hachette Book
Group supports the right to free ex-
pression and the value of copyright.
The purpose of copyright is to encourage
writers and artists to produce the creative
works that enrich our culture. • The scan-
ning, uploading, and distribution of this book
without permission is a theft of the author's in-
tellectual property. If you would like permission to
use material from the book (other than for review pur-
poses), please contact permissions@hbgusa.com. Thank
you for your support of the author's rights. • Little, Brown
and Company • Hachette Book Group • 1290 Avenue of the
Americas, New York, NY 10104 • Visit us at LBYR.com • First
Edition: April 2018 • Little, Brown and Company is a division of
Hachette Book Group, Inc. The Little, Brown name and logo are trade-
marks of Hachette Book Group, Inc. • The publisher is not responsible for
websites (or their content) that are not owned by the publisher. • Library of
Congress Cataloging-in-Publication Data • Names: Blackall, Sophie, author. •
Title: Hello Lighthouse / by Sophie Blackall. • Description: First Edition. | New
York : Little, Brown and Company, 2018. | Summary: "Explores the life of one light-
house as it beams its message out to sea through shifting seasons, changeable weather, and
the tenure of its final keeper." —Provided by publisher. • Identifiers: LCCN 2016046016 |
ISBN 9780316362382 (hardcover) | ISBN 9780316362375 (ebook) | ISBN 9780316362344 (li-
brary edition ebook) • Subjects: | CYAC: Lighthouses—Fiction.• Classification: LCC PZ7.B5319 Hel
2018 | DDC [E]—dc23 • LC record available at https://lccn.loc.gov/2016046016 • ISBNs: 978-0-316-
36238-2 (hardcover), 978-0-316-36237-5 (ebook), 978-0-316-51903-8 (ebook), 978-0-316-51905-2 (ebook) •
PRINTED IN CHINA • APS • 10 9 8 7 6 5 4 3 2 1

For Susan Rich—editor, friend, beacon of light

HELLO LIGHTHOUSE

Sophie Blackall

L B
Little, Brown and Company
New York Boston

On the highest rock of a tiny island
at the edge of the world stands a lighthouse.
It is built to last forever.
Sending its light out to sea,
guiding the ships on their way.

From dusk to dawn, the lighthouse beams.
Hello!
…Hello!
…Hello!
Hello, Lighthouse!

The new keeper arrives to replace the old,
to carry on tending the light.
He polishes the lens and refills the oil
and trims the burned end of the wick.
Throughout the night, he winds the clockwork
that keeps the lamp in motion.
During the day, he gives the round rooms a fresh
coat of sea-green paint.
He writes in the logbook and threads his needle
and listens to the gathering wind.

The wind takes a deep breath and blows and blows.

Hello!

...Hello!

...H e l l o !

The keeper boils water and drinks his tea,
as he fishes for cod from the window.
He sets the table and hums a tune and wishes
for someone to talk to.

Every few days he writes her a letter
and throws it into the waves.
He tends the light and writes in the logbook
and waits for her reply.

The sky grows dark, and the waves rise and crash.
HELLO!
...HELLO!
...HELLO!

The keeper looks through his telescope.
The tender arrives, bringing oil and flour
and pork and beans…

…and his wife.

He shows her around
the round rooms
of their house.
He tends the light
and writes in the logbook
and sets the table for two.

The fog makes everything disappear.
A bell must be rung to warn the ships!
Clang!
…Clang!
…Clang!

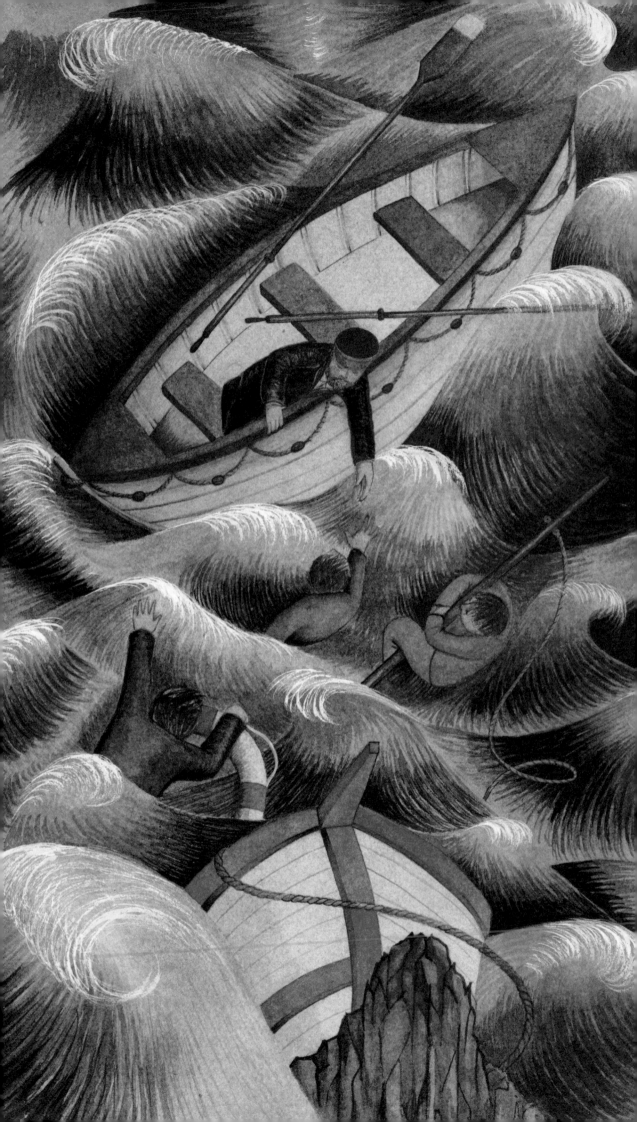

One thick night, disaster strikes!
A boat is wrecked on the rocks!
Not a moment to lose, the keeper rows out.
He pulls three sailors from the deep, black sea.
He tends the light and writes in the logbook
and wraps the sailors in blankets.

The sea turns into a carpet of ice.
Hello!
…Hello!
…Hello!

One dawn, the keeper begins to sneeze;
by dusk he is terribly ill.

His wife is
        e v e r y w h e r e
            all at once,

                    running ^{up} and _{down} spiral stairs.

She tends the light
and feeds him broth
and chips ice
off the lantern room windows.
She sits by his side
and writes in the logbook
the minute his fever breaks.

The icebergs pass by on their journey south.
The whales pass by on their journey north.
Hello!
…Hello!
…Hello!

Inside the lighthouse, the woman walks around and around the room. Her husband boils water and helps her breathe in—

and out. He tends the light and writes in the logbook...

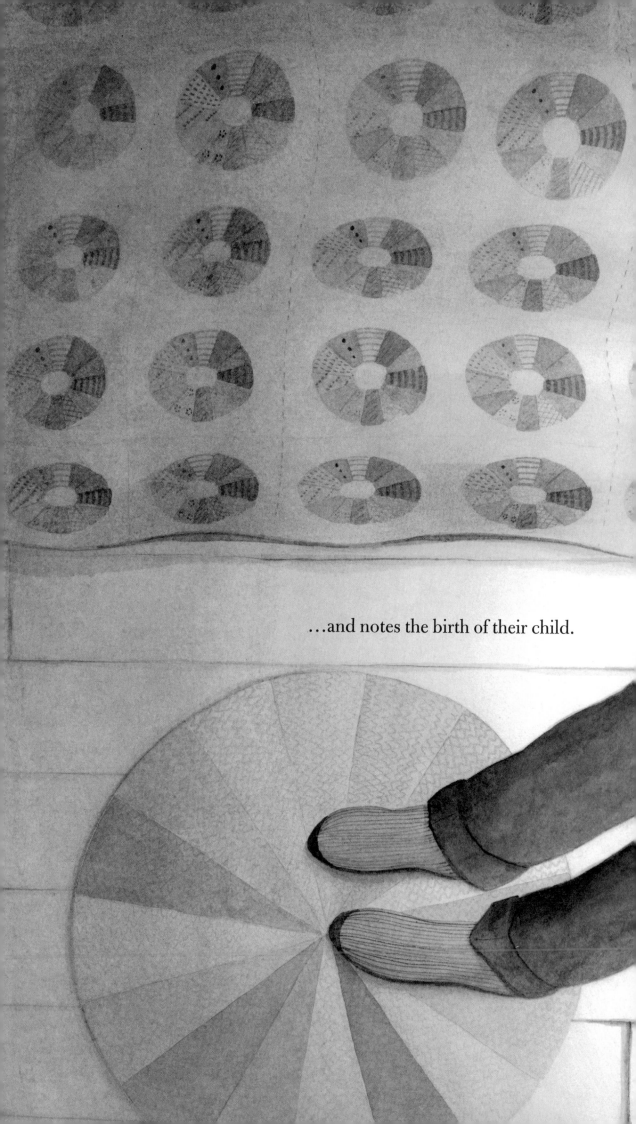

...and notes the birth of their child.

The sky erupts in swirls of green.
Hello!
…Hello!
…Hello!

The tender arrives, bringing oil and
flour and pork and beans
and the mail.

Along with fresh books and news from the land,
there's an unexpected letter
with the coast guard's seal.
The keeper winds the clockwork and polishes
the lens, just as he's always done.
He tends the light and writes in the logbook,
but knows that it's not for long.

Together they watch the horizon.

The coast guard arrives
with a brand-new light
and installs the machine to run it.

No lamp to fill,
no wick to trim.
The keeper's work is done.

He climbs to the top
of the spiral stairs
and closes the logbook
for good.

They pack their belongings
into the boat
and wave farewell
to the gulls.

Beyond the breakers, they all look up.
Good-bye, Lighthouse!
Good-bye!
...Good-bye!
...Good-bye!

On the highest rock of a tiny island
at the edge of the world stands a lighthouse.
It is built to last forever.
Sending its light out to sea.

The fog rolls in, and the fog rolls out.
The waves rise and crash.
The wind blows and blows.
                Hello!
                  …Hello!
                    …*Hello?*

ABOUT LIGHTHOUSES

I USED TO THINK of lighthouses from the point of view of a ship: the faithful sentinel standing tall, beaming its light out to sea, warning of dangerous rocks, guiding sailors to safety. But one day I was at a flea market and an old print showing a cutaway interior of a lighthouse jumped out at me. The drawing made me think of what it would be like to live inside a lighthouse, to make my home in those tiny round rooms, miles from land, all alone. I delved into research, looked at pictures, read books, visited museums, and climbed the towers of lighthouses from New York to Newfoundland.

I learned that the keeper's job was to tend the light from sunset to sunrise and to never, ever let it go out. Sometimes a keeper had an assistant, someone to play checkers with and help share the night watch. They did not always get along. One keeper and his assistant apparently annoyed each other so much that they went a year without speaking and ate all their meals facing in opposite directions. Often families lived together on lighthouses; some had as many as eleven children. Hundreds of women served as lighthouse keepers. Some replaced a husband or father, but many were appointed for the job.

Several times during the night, the keepers would have to wake up and wind the clockwork that turned the lens. They would trim the burned ends of the wick and fill the lamp with oil, which they carried in a heavy bucket from the tank in the cellar all the way up the spiral stairs. They kept the lens free of dust so it would shine brightly, polishing the soot away each morning. Curtains were drawn on sunny days to prevent a fire in the lens. The lantern room windows had to be kept spotlessly clean. In winter, this meant chipping away ice, which was a dangerous job. The keepers held tight to special handles attached to the outside, and sometimes tied themselves to the railing so they wouldn't be blown away in strong winds.

In foggy weather, a signal was sounded to warn ships when the light could not be seen. In the early days the keepers did this by hand, striking a bell with a hammer every twenty seconds, which would have been exhausting, not to mention loud. In time, these were replaced by clockwork bells and, in larger lighthouses, steam-driven foghorns. Some lighthouse keepers learned to sleep through the din of the horn; others nearly went mad when the fog lasted for days.

There was constant maintenance keeping the saltwater-and-wind-battered lighthouse freshly painted, along with the usual household jobs—washing, cooking, mending, and stoking the coal stove. Water was pumped from the tank by hand. Waste from kitchen slops and chamber pots was thrown into the sea.

Everything that happened had to be meticulously recorded each day in a logbook: little things like the weather, how much oil was used, and which ships passed by, as well as big things like births and deaths and shipwrecks.

But even with all these daily chores, there was lots of spare time to fill. Keepers read books and played solitaire, knitted and embroidered, made model ships or tiny lighthouses to pass the quiet hours. Some keepers made kites to fly from the lantern gallery, or fished to supplement the tedious dinners of beans. Others brought seeds and sacks of dirt from the mainland to plant gardens in among the rock pools.

Everything the keeper needed had to be brought from shore by a supply ship called a tender. The tender came every few months and brought the oil to run the lamp. It brought food to last a season (mostly canned and dried) and water in barrels for drinking and washing (collected rainwater was never enough). The tender